Visit with a Mermaid

for Alexis

Visit with a Mermaid

STORY AND PICTURES BY
Pierre Le-Tan

Clarkson N. Potter, Inc. / *Publishers*
Distributed by Crown Publishers, Inc.
New York

First American Edition published by Clarkson N. Potter, Inc.
One Park Avenue, New York, New York 10016
and simultaneously in Canada by General Publishing Company Limited
Manufactured in the United States of America
Originally published in France in 1981 by Hachette

10 9 8 7 6 5 4 3 2 1
First Edition

Library of Congress Cataloging in Publication Data

Le-Tan, Pierre.
  Visit with a mermaid.

  Translation of: Voyage avec la sirène.
  Summary: On the beach, Olympia is befriended by a
red-haired mermaid named Louise who introduces her to
her underwater friends.
  [1. Fantasy. 2. Mermaids—Fiction] I. Title.
PZ7.L566Vi 1982 [E]   82-15149
ISBN 0-517-54894-1

Here is Olympia. She is spending
her vacation by the seashore.

"Be good," her mother says.
"I'm going on an errand with Alex. We'll be back soon."

But Olympia is too busy making sand castles to reply.

A lady with red hair waves to Olympia. "Come and see me," she says. "There's nothing to be afraid of. Put on your yellow rubber duck."

Olympia wades into the water.

"What is that big fish behind you?" Olympia asks.

"It's my tail," she says. "I'm a mermaid. My name is Louise. Would you like to come see my island?"

Louise lives on a little island near the beach. She leads a peaceful life there. When she is hungry, she goes underwater to pick some seaweed.

"Today I wanted company," Louise says, "so I came to see you."

Louise has a wonderful collection of
seashells from oceans all over the world.
Olympia holds a large shell from Australia to
her ear. She can hear kangaroos jumping.

   "Would you like to go to the bottom
of the sea?" asks Louise. "I can give you
the magical power to breathe underwater."

Here they are diving to the bottom of the sea. The mermaid has many friends underwater.

"Hello, Louise!" say the fish.

Here is the Benson family.
The big fish wearing glasses is the old
schoolteacher, Mr. Porter.

Louise and Olympia go to visit Paul and Susan, who are watching a gangster movie on television. Olympia plays with Sophie, their daughter.

"Come and see my toys," Sophie says to Olympia.

Olympia has never seen fish-dolls before!
Isn't it funny? Sophie has the same trumpet
that Alex has at home.

Who is this frightening creature
coming out from under a rock?
Olympia and Sophie don't bother to ask him
his name. They swim off to find Louise.

"Look, I've found a beautiful shell for you,"
says Louise. "Now let's go back to the beach."
Olympia holds on to the mermaid's tail
and waves good-bye to Sophie.
"See you again soon, I hope."

Mother has brought back a chocolate ice-cream cone for Olympia.

"Where did you find this lovely shell?" she asks.

"It's a secret," says Olympia.

Across the water on the little island, Olympia's duck rests quietly.

A note to parents:

As every parent knows, children love fantasy but also need to know exactly what is true and what is not true. Please make sure your child knows that he must not wade out into the water as Olympia did, and that real children cannot be given the power to breathe underwater! *Visit with a Mermaid* is strictly make-believe.

The Editor

Visit with a Mermaid

was designed by Katy Homans

and handset in Monotype Dante by Michael & Winifred Bixler